FIRST BASE,
FIRST PLACE

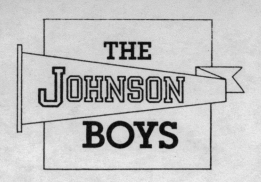

THE JOHNSON BOYS

FIRST BASE, FIRST PLACE

SCOTT ELLER

AN
APPLE
PAPERBACK

SCHOLASTIC INC.
New York Toronto London Auckland Sydney

ISBN 0-590-42827-6

12 11 10 9 8 7 6 5 4 3 2 1   3 4 5 6 7/9

Printed in the U.S.A.   28

First Scholastic printing, April 1993

Contents

FIRST BASE,
FIRST PLACE

Prologue

The baseball diamond had been abandoned for five months, lying dormant day after cold day under the gray winter sky. But today the temperature was 42 degrees, the sun shone brightly, the cloudless sky was an intense blue, and the breeze blowing steadily off the Long Island Sound was almost warm.

In the shade of the backstop behind home plate, the last of the snow was turning to water. Beneath the bleachers, tattered paper cups and faded gum wrappers dropped by last summer's fans littered the brown grass. In the outfield, robins hunted excitedly for worms. A cardinal sang from high up in the oak tree that stood beyond the right field fence, and if you looked closely at the ancient tree's lower branches where two sparrows were chasing one another from twig to twig, you could see at the end of each crooked branch a fresh green bud.

It was a Saturday morning in late March. Spring was only a few days old.

A car pulled to a stop in the parking lot behind the diamond and a man got out. The car door slammed, and the man walked over to the field. He was tall and wore jeans, a blue jacket, and a Boston Red Sox cap tilted back on his head. Walkman earphones hung around his neck. He paused near the pitcher's mound, stuck his hands into his back pockets, and looked around. The muddy infield was marked with deep footprints, and there were wet depressions where the bases belonged. The outfield was bumpy and rough from having been frozen and thawed over and over, all winter long, and the grass was stiff and brown, with spots of green scattered here and there. A good-sized patch of left field was submerged beneath a miniature lake.

The breeze nudged the collar of the tall man's jacket and pushed around a few dry leaves, left over from the previous fall.

The man leaned back, gazed up at the sky, and inhaled deeply. Then he abruptly turned and trudged back to his car. From its trunk he retrieved a large cardboard box full of tools and equipment. He carried the box back over to the baseball diamond and placed it on the bench in the home-team dugout. From out of the box he took a dusty canvas object with two spikes dangling from it and a claw hammer; carrying these, he trudged back over to the muddy infield. He sighted along the foul line toward home plate, then turned and gazed out toward the center of the infield. He squinted. Then he took two or three comical sidesteps; someone observing him, not knowing what he was doing, might have thought he was reading a treasure map and looking for the exact place to dig for buried gold and jewels.

Finally, he knelt down on one knee and arranged third base square to the foul line and the base path. He started knocking one of the steel spikes, to which the base was attached with a heavy cotton strap, into the soft clay. The earphones around his neck swung down and tapped him under the chin. He stood up, carefully removed them, and put them away in his jacket pocket. Then he knelt down again and continued driving the stake into the ground.

The *tink, tink, tink* of the hammerhead striking the steel spike echoed off the houses that faced the park. People in the houses — kids, parents, retired couples, young couples sleeping late — people either still in bed or eating breakfast or watching Saturday morning cartoons or reading the morning paper in the homes near the diamond looked up from what they were doing. Some of them recognized the sound, which they hadn't heard for five long months, and smiled to themselves. They knew the meaning of the sound: A new season was beginning.

1.
Summer League

"**C**ome on, Mom, we're gonna be late!"

Gabriel Fixx was playing tug-of-war with Duhe, his big Newfoundland, in the small yard in front of his house. The lawn was full and green; Gabriel had mown the grass three times already this spring.

Duhe was tugging for all he was worth on the shredded towel, but Gabriel, digging the heels of his high-tops into the lawn, easily held his own. Although Duhe was powerful, Gabriel was big and strong for his age, and the dog was no match for him.

"Okay, boy, you ready?" Gabriel asked grinning, and Duhe let out an excited growl.

Gabriel released the towel.

Duhe tumbled backward, paws flailing, and bounced right back onto his feet. He bounded toward Gabriel, who crouched to receive the full force of Duhe's charge, tackling the big dog and wrestling him to the ground. The two of them rolled across the lawn.

"Gabe?"

They stopped playing and looked up. Gabriel's mother stood by the front door.

"Yeah, Mom?"

"I thought practice wasn't till eleven."

Gabriel balled up the towel and winged it. Duhe charged after it.

"I wanted to get there early. It's our last practice before the first game."

Gabriel's mom raised her eyebrows. "You want to get there an *hour* early?"

"I was going to meet the guys — they were going to get there early, too."

"Let me guess which guys."

Gabriel laughed. "Bet you eleven thousand, five hundred dollars you can't." He picked up the towel Duhe had dropped at his feet and tossed it again.

"Don't tell me. Could it be . . . Pik and Andy and Ray?"

"Guess I'm out eleven thousand, five hundred."

She came and stood beside him. Duhe bounded over with the towel; they watched him hunker down on his stomach in the grass and begin happily chewing.

"You four really are planning on winning this year, aren't you?" Gabriel's mother asked.

He nodded. "We've talked about it a lot. We

6

don't think there's much point in planning anything else."

"So are you guys the big stars? The four of you, I mean."

Gabriel shrugged. "Maybe."

"Think the rest of your teammates are up to winning a championship?"

"I don't know," Gabriel replied. "Andy and Pik and Ray and I want it. I'm not so sure about the other guys."

"But because you four are the best, you have to get there an hour early?" She pulled his hair playfully.

He laughed. But when he spoke, he wasn't kidding. "How do you think we got to be so good?"

She nodded. "Okay, come on. I'm ready to go when you are."

He started to say something, but she beat him to it: "Okay," she said, "we'll give the other stars a ride, too."

Twenty minutes later, he was sitting on the bench in the dugout, lacing his spikes and talking to Andy and Pik. Ray was late. The day was perfect for baseball: the temperature was up in the sixties, the sun was high in the sky, and a slight breeze was blowing out toward center.

Andy was staring at Gabriel's glove, which was lying on the bench next to him. "What *is* this?"

he asked, picking it up. "Butt steak?"

"Hey, what happened?" Pik reached out a long arm and grabbed the glove out of Andy's hand. "Your mom stick this in the disposal or something?"

Gabriel laughed. He finished tying his laces and sat up. "Duhe got ahold of it."

"Man!" said Andy. "Look at those teeth marks!"

"A glove with teeth," Pik said. "Just what he needs."

"What's that, a spider?" Gabriel said to Pik, pointing.

"What?" Pik looked down at his shirt.

"Facial!" Gabriel flipped his hand up in Pik's face, smacking him.

"Mutant Ninja says *die!*" Pik shouted, and he grabbed Gabriel around the head and flung him onto the grass. The two of them rolled and tumbled toward the on-deck circle. Andy leaped on top of them with a scream: *"Yaaaaaaaaaaaaaaa!"*

Gabriel struggled to his feet and ran over to the bench. Pik and Andy were wrestling, shouting and laughing; Pik, the bigger of the two, was starting to get the better of Andy. Gabriel pawed through the contents of Pik's Adidas bag — batting glove, can of glove oil, towel, wallet, gum wrappers, sweatshirt, CDs (CDs?). . . . He grabbed Pik's wallet and slipped it into his own bag.

Pik had just about pinned Andy. Andy was twisting and wriggling, trying to break loose when Gabriel yelled, "Rickie Henderson!" as he ran and slid headfirst into the pile.

Ray showed up and joined in by yelling, "Death from Above!" and flopping on Gabriel's back. They pounded on each other for a few minutes until a voice interrupted them:

"I could use a hand with the equipment here."

They sat up, blinking. "Coach!"

"Hey Coach!"

Coach Morris stood over them, looking down. He tugged at his Boston Red Sox cap, then gestured with his thumb over his shoulder, pointing toward the parking lot. "There's a bag of balls, and bats, and the box with the bases in it, over in the trunk of my car."

"Balls, bats, bases, boxes, and bags," Andy chanted.

"Aren't there child-labor laws?" said Pik.

They hauled the equipment from the parking lot to the dugout, then helped Coach line up the three bases. Gabriel, standing over the bag at second, kept knocking it out of line with his feet, and Coach finally told them all to go warm up, he'd get the bases down.

Other players began arriving. Silent Mike MacDonald rode up on his rusty twelve-speed, and Ronnie Duggan, the catcher they called, "fire-

9

plug," was dropped off by his mother. Best friends Steve Wright and Tony Picarazzi arrived together, wheeling noisily across the parking lot on skateboards. Ray watched them all arrive, standing off by himself. He was big and quiet and minded his own business, playing baseball with a kind of serious concentration. Gabriel wondered if he were still friendly with his former teammates on Flood. He'd never really asked.

As a team, they'd been playing for seven weeks now, practicing on Wednesday afternoons and Saturday mornings. Coach Morris, never without his Red Sox cap or Walkman, had put the team through drill after drill, day after day. There were drills for defense — pop flies, grounders, throwing to different bases, cutting off a throw to the plate, and firing to second or third; and there were drills for offense — hitting to the opposite field, the hit-and-run, bunting, stealing second, stealing home. The guys were used to the drills by now, and good at them. They were beginning to look like a team.

Coach signaled the beginning of practice and everybody gathered near home plate to run bases, always the first drill. They lined up in the order they batted: Andy first; Gabriel second; then Ray; Pik next, batting clean-up; and so on down the line.

10

"Go!" Coach yelled, and Andy sprinted toward first. As he rounded the bag, Coach shouted "Go!" again, and Gabriel took off. He swung right, onto the grass in foul territory, and rounded first at full speed. He knew he'd never catch Andy, but he always tried. As he rounded second and dug for third, an idea hit him. He cut across the infield grass toward home. Andy saw him coming. The rest of the team, standing around home waiting their turn, scattered.

Andy, laughing, slid feet first; Gabriel dove headfirst. The collision knocked over a few of the guys Pik called scrubeenies, frail guys who usually had trouble getting out of the way.

Gabriel and Andy lay around laughing.

Coach wasn't. He chewed them out.

"There goes my comedy career," Gabriel said, lying on home plate and dusting himself off.

Coach ignored him. "Listen up, fellas," he said, "I've been thinking about some changes in the batting order."

"What do you mean?" said Gabriel. He pulled himself up to his knees. Andy was still sitting, testing his tongue for dirt.

Coach looked around. He had everyone's attention. "I'm going to try out something new. Duggan's been showing some power, so I thought I'd put him in the clean-up spot for now. Ray's hitting well so I'm leaving him in the third spot. That way they can't pitch around Ray, knowing Duggan's on deck. Now Fixx, you done screwing around?"

Gabriel could see Pik staring at the coach in disbelief, and he knew Pik did not appreciate getting knocked out of the clean-up spot by Duggan, of all people.

"I don't know, Coach," Gabriel said. He opened his mouth and stuck his tongue out, grabbing his stomach. He doubled over. "I don't feel so good all of a sudden."

"What now?" Coach sounded exasperated.

Gabriel took a few staggering steps toward the bench. He was limping, clutching his stomach. Some of the guys started laughing. He stumbled over to the bench and fell on top of his gym bag. Lying across the bag, so no one could see, he dug around in it. Then he started gagging and retching, pretending to vomit.

"Gross!" someone hollered. "Don't yak on my shoes!"

Gabriel gave a big, loud heave, holding his hands in front of his face, and laid a big pile in the grass.

Andy rolled his eyes. Pik shook his head.

Ray said, "Call the color for fifty cents! I got green!"

Coach Morris walked over to Gabriel, hands on his hips.

"Gag me," kids were saying in the background.

"Always a classic," Andy said. "The old rubber-vomit trick."

Coach Morris picked up the rubber vomit and flipped it into the wind. It sailed like a Frisbee.

The kids all watched it, laughing.

"Hey," Gabriel said. "The old flying rubber-vomit trick."

"Come on, Fixx," Coach said, "get with it. We've got work to do here."

Gabriel looked up at him. He could tell Coach was trying not to laugh.

Coach said, "Ever hear about the kid who cried 'Wolf'?"

"That's right," said Gabriel. "Someday I'll really vomit and then you'll pick it up to throw it."

Coach Morris cracked a smile — one of the few they'd seen all spring. "Listen up now!" he said after the laughter died down. "Our first game against Law — in case you've forgotten — is less than a week away, and we're not ready. Let's get some work done today. Come on. Bunting drill. Let's go!"

Loose, now, and ready to practice, the team settled down to work. They went to Johnson Junior High, on the blue-collar side of town, and they were proud of it. It gave them added motivation, knowing that the snobs across town looked down at them. Those other kids — the Polo-shirt crowd at Flood — had two hundred dollar gloves; played on a raked, rolled, and manicured diamond — and got new uniforms every year. So the Johnson kids practiced longer and harder. A win over Flood was never easy — and was always what they wanted most.

After the practice was over, and everyone had gone home, including Coach, Gabriel and Andy and Pik played for another hour. Ray had to help out at home, so he took off. Gabriel pitched to Andy, and then he pitched to Pik. They switched positions, and Andy pitched to Gabriel while Pik roamed the outfield, shagging flies. Then they moved to the infield and practiced defense. They were sweating, and exhausted, and hungry and thirsty, but they were loving every minute of it — laughing, hooting, and keeping track of dropped fly balls, missed grounders, and overthrows.

Finally, they went back to the bench. They took off their spikes and put on sneaks. They stripped off their wet shirts and put on dry ones.

"How are we getting home?" Andy asked.

"Walking," Gabriel said.

"Oh man," Andy sighed. "We should've ridden our bikes."

"Naw," said Pik. He was rummaging around in his Adidas bag. "Hey! Where's my wallet?"

"Lose something?" said Gabriel. He was fiddling with his baseball glove.

Andy pulled his wallet out of his gym bag. "Here's mine, man." He fumbled it, and change dropped on the ground by their feet.

"Nice move, Ace," said Pik. "Great hands for a shortstop."

Andy ducked down and began picking up his change.

"Really, no kidding," said Pik. "Who's got the goods here? I need that wallet."

"Don't look at me," said Gabriel, still tightening the laces on his glove.

Andy was busy on the ground in front of the bench.

"Come on, you two!" said Pik. "That sucker didn't grow legs!"

Andy stood up. He snatched Gabriel's bag and ran.

"Hey!" Gabriel shouted. He threw down his glove and went after him. He took only half a step, then fell flat on his face.

Andy had tied the laces of Gabriel's high-tops together.

Pik cracked up.

Andy was standing over by the on-deck circle. He dug around in Gabriel's bag, then held up Pik's wallet triumphantly. "Beat Flood!" he yelled.

Then, his face aimed at the sky, he screamed as loud as he could: "BEAT FLOOD!"

His voice frightened pigeons that had been scrounging meals behind the wooden bleachers; and they rose into the late-afternoon sunlight, flapping wildly, as they swooped across the bright green diamond.

2.
The Practice

Early on the morning of the opening game against Jonathan Law, Andy and Gabriel and Ray rode their bikes through a drizzle to Pik's house. When they got there, Pik met them at the door, looking glum.

"Mom has the car," he said. "We gotta wait."

They followed him into the kitchen and sat at the table arguing about the Jonathan Law pitcher, while Pik stood by the window, directing and re-directing an ant across the formica counter near the sink.

Pik's father came into the kitchen, got a can of A&W cream soda out of the refrigerator without speaking to any of them, and walked back out again.

"We oughta get rid of that hunka junk," Pik said suddenly, loudly. His father kept going. Pik's comments were directed at the Telanders' second car, visible from the kitchen window.

Ray snorted. Gabriel and Andy looked at each

17

other and grinned. The yellow Buick was so spotted with rust that its sides looked machine-gunned. It squatted out in the yard in the rain where it always stood. None of them could remember when it had ever worked, but Pik's father refused to regard it with anything but fondness. "That automobile doesn't owe me anything," he said from the den, where he had taken up his usual seat in the recliner, staring at the wall as if it were television, his soda resting on one massive thigh.

Pik shrugged.

"It's raining," said his father. "If I drive you over to the game, and it's rained out, I'm not waiting around."

"Thanks, Dad," said Pik. To Andy and Gabriel and Ray he said, "It's still an hour to game time. Let's go upstairs."

Sometimes, when they had time on their hands, the four of them played a ferocious game of Nerf basketball on their knees against Pik's bedroom door — now cracked in two places as a result of their intense play. But today they were too keyed up.

Ray wandered over to what they called the War Wall — a floor-to-ceiling bookcase filled with the only kind of books Pik read: nonfiction books on war, mostly the Second World War. Pik thumped down nervously on the end of his bed, flapping his feet. Gabriel went to the fifty-gallon terrarium and lifted up Heinrich, Pik's pet iguana. Andy stood at the window, as if to accelerate Pik's mom's arrival.

Gabriel raised Heinrich to eye level. "Hey, Heiny."

"Careful," said Andy. "He bites."

"Only people he doesn't like, like you, Android. He likes me, don't you, Heiny?"

"Yeah, Gabriel. Everybody likes you. Even lizards," Andy shot back.

Pik yawned. Heinrich opened and closed his mouth.

"He's hungry," Ray said.

"No. Put him down. He's telling you he's starting to get annoyed," said Pik.

Andy jeered as Gabriel hastily put Heinrich back in his terrarium.

"Car to starboard," said Andy, looking out through the drizzle. "It's your mom, Pik."

Pik bounded off the bed. "C'mon. My father can drive us. Now, let's get movin'."

They could see from a block away that the field was empty. As the car entered the parking lot, mud splashed everywhere. Pik's father stopped singing weird old songs like one called, "Fat and Greasy," long enough to look at them significantly as he pulled behind the backstop.

19

"Let's go," said Pik, throwing the car door open.

Pik's father shook his head, lowered his chin, and bounced a little with a silent burp. "All right. I'll see you at five," he said.

They all splashed over to the visitors' dugout and took their seats on the damp bench.

"I think it's letting up," Andy said, hopefully, as the rain continued.

"Right," Ray said. He looked up, completely soaked.

The dugout smelled of damp wood and dirt. The puddles in the infield were spreading into one another and long stretches of the outfield were beginning to look like the Everglades.

Andy shook his head, remembering the hard time his father had given him lately about how all these sports cut into study time. His father pictured Andy in pre-med at Berkeley in about five years. All Andy could see was himself as shortstop in the College World Series, lying on a beach somewhere when he wasn't turning double plays.

Well, it was a long way from the beach today.

Beside him, Ray was methodically changing into his spikes, careful not to put his stockinged feet down in the mud. Then he put on his batting glove and wristband. Gabriel took his Kevin Mitchell bat, and began to do wrist exercises with it.

"Nobody's coming," Pik said.

Gabriel kept twirling his bat. "Maybe not."

Andy reached for his spikes. Finally, reluctantly, Pik did, too.

"I say we do fielding drills," Andy said.

They looked at him, making him feel like a lost ball in high grass.

"*Fielding* drills?" Pik repeated.

"Well what do you want to do? We're here. We gonna just sit here, waiting for the sun?"

"Let's give 'em another minute," Gabriel suggested. "Maybe they'll show up."

"We're like Charlie Brown or something," Pik said. "Pathetic. It's kinda depressing. I mean, if we can't play, what're we doing here?"

"All right then," Ray said to Pik. "Let's do it."

"Hey!" Gabriel exclaimed. "Look at that dog in the rain."

Andy leaned out of the dugout. The next thing he knew, he'd been tackled. He went down on the third-base line with a huge splash, skidding halfway to the pitcher's mound.

"What're you doing? Are you nuts?" Andy yelled, as he began to get up. But Gabriel tackled him again, rolling him through the mud.

"You're nuts!" Andy got Gabriel in a headlock, splashing mud and water on his face. Gabriel pulled free, and stood looking a second at Andy, the mud making long dark streaks down his face. Then he took off for second base from the third-base side and dove headfirst, splitting the puddles into muddy spray, and sliding all the way over second base. He stood up with a whoop and took off for first.

"You guys are just *very* immature," Ray said.

"Pete Rose!" shouted Andy, scrambling to his feet. He took off after Gabriel. "Pete Rose, Pete Rose!" and he flung himself into first base — body stretched, hands reaching for the bag, a real Pete Rose slide.

"Frankenball," gasped Andy. He got up and held his arms out in front of himself like in a Frankenstein movie, and headed for the dugout and Pik and Ray. Gabriel followed.

Pik scooted sideways, dodging the water, now coming through the leaks in the dugout. Gabriel grabbed Ray's arms, Andy got his legs, and they hauled him out into the mud.

Halfway to the pitcher's mound, a surprise tackle by Pik brought them all down.

"Play ball!" howled Pik, and grabbed the second-base bag. Using it as a football, they played round-robin.

The rain was still falling when Pik's father finally showed up.

"Hey!" he shouted. "Hey! Don't even think

about getting in this car like that!"

But he waited, with the engine running, as Gabriel ran across home plate holding the second-base bag high over his head: Touchdown. Final score, three to two to two.

3.
Coach

So their opening game was against Flood at Flood.

After they'd warmed up, right before the game started, Coach sat them all down on the bench in the dugout and went over signs and strategy.

The whole time Coach was talking, Ray sat there with his eyes closed, getting ready. Pik glared over toward the Flood dugout, as if he could psyche them out. As if they could even see him, thought Gabriel.

Andy watched the rest of his team out of the corner of his eye. They were not what he would call pumped up — which didn't help.

Gabriel made a show of listening to Coach, but he'd heard it all before. He's a nice guy, Gabriel told himself. Then somewhere inside a voice answered: Nice guys finish last.

"Any questions?" Coach concluded.

Nobody said anything right away.

"All right," Coach began, fiddling with his

Walkman earphones, but then Pik's hand slowly went up.

"Pik?" Coach nodded, earphones ready.

Andy leaned forward. This'll be good, he thought. You never knew what Pik was going to say, but when he did say something at times like this, it was usually a bomb.

This time he said, "What about losing to Flood last year?"

Gabriel registered what Pik had said about two seconds later.

But Coach didn't even seemed fazed. "Well, what about it?"

"Are you gonna say anything about it? About beating them this season?"

"I hadn't thought about it exactly, no. Why?"

Pik shrugged, a big, elaborate, really snide shrug. "Gee whiz Coach, I dunno. You're the coach. I just thought we were here to win. That's all."

Pik's sarcasm finally got through to Coach. He frowned and thrust his chin forward. "Telander, you're here to play. Winning isn't everything. You play as hard as you can, every one of you. Play up to your ability. I don't ask more than that. We're here for fun as well as for winning."

Ray said, "Winning's more fun."

Everyone stared at him. But Coach wasn't going to be baited any further.

"Everyone who comes to practice, plays. We'll win some, and maybe we'll lose some. But win or lose, we're a team, and on a real team, everybody's as important as everybody else.

Now get out there and hustle." He popped the earphones in place, sat down on the dugout bench and folded his arms.

"Case closed," Gabriel muttered to Andy. But it wasn't Andy trotting alongside his left shoulder, it was Duggan.

"Maybe it's the reason he never made the majors," Gabriel said. "You know? He didn't get it about winning."

Duggan didn't answer. He just kept trotting past Gabriel, out to his position behind the plate. It made Gabriel feel like a Mutant Ninja nerd.

Gabriel toed the mound, started his practice pitches, thumping the ball into Duggan's mitt. That guy, he thought. Bad enough, with Coach. But Duggan's definitely got an attitude.

Flood went ahead in the first inning and stayed there, 5–1. By the fifth, Gabriel and Pik were 0-for-1 and Andy was 0-for-2. The only run had come from Duggan. He homered to left, his first time at bat, really cranked it, then trotted past the infield as if they were invisible.

But then, thought Gabriel, he didn't pay too much attention to his own team, either.

"Hey!" Coach pulled the earphones loose, as if

that would help Gabriel hear better. "Wake up, Gabriel. You're up."

Gabriel jumped up, grabbed his bat. Behind him Andy began to chant softly, then louder and louder: "Frozen rope, frozen rope, frozen rope."

Digging in with his spikes, Gabriel crouched over the plate. This kid's no good, he thought. His pitches are nothing. C'mon wimp. C'mon. C'mon. . . .

The pitcher let fly. Gabriel stepped into it and lined it; a true frozen rope, a shot so hard it would have torn the second baseman's glove off — if he'd had the time to lift it. Gabriel made it to second, standing up.

"Righteous!" yelled Andy, at the top of his lungs. "Sincere!"

Even Ray said "Yeah."

Across the diamond, Flood's relief pitcher uncoiled, stood up, ambled around behind the dugout, and began to warm up.

The Mantis. Their best reliever, with a sidearm motion that looked like he'd wrench his arm off; pitches that left his insect-fingered hand looking easy and slow — *until* they came over the plate . . . anywhere your bat wasn't. They hoped he wasn't coming in anytime soon.

"C'mon Ray," muttered Gabriel.

Ray took the first pitch; a fat, low giveaway strike.

"C'*mon*," said Gabriel.

Another pitch just touching the outside of the plate — strike two, and Ray hadn't taken the bat off his shoulder.

The third pitch just floated toward the plate. Ray stepped into it and swung all the way from the soles of his feet. The ball lashed into the right-field corner, rebounded past the right fielder, and kept rolling. By the time the Flood player had gotten his glove on it, Gabriel had scored — still standing up — and Ray was on third.

And the score was now 5–2.

"Excellent!" Andy was screaming as Gabriel trotted past Duggan, taking his warm-up swings, and into the dugout, low-fiving his teammates. Coach nodded.

Out on the mound, the Flood coach was talking to his starting pitcher. He left him there, either to give the Mantis a chance to warm up more, or because he was part of the everybody-gets-to-play mentality, too.

Gabriel caught Andy's eye. Then they both leaned forward as the Flood starter wound up.

Ball one.

Ball two.

"Wait for your pitch," shouted Coach.

Duggan slammed it, a screaming homer to the same spot as before, driving Pik home, and coasting around the bases like he hit two home runs a game everyday.

Gabriel was screaming with the rest of the team, pounding on Ray and Duggan as they came in. But he noticed that Duggan didn't even seem to care.

Attitude, he thought.

But now it was 5–4. The Flood coach came out. The Flood pitcher walked off without even waiting for his coach to reach him. And the Mantis took the mound.

Pik went down on three pitches, swinging at air.

Then Mike MacDonald, followed by Steve Wright. Three up, three down.

"Using that famous *invisible bat*, again, MacDonald?" asked Pik.

Mike turned red, but it was Ronnie Duggan who headed for Pik.

Gabriel grabbed Ronnie's arm. "Forget it, Duggan."

Duggan tried to jerk free, just once, to prove he was serious, then turned away, still scowling.

"Hey, hey," Coach said, catching on a little late. "This is a game here, you know. Let's keep our heads in it."

"Game's on the field," said Ray, as much to Coach as the rest of the guys.

"C'mon," said Andy. "Let's hold 'em."

But Gabriel couldn't. He walked the first kid, a giant of a kid with a fifty foot strike zone, practically. Now Duggan came out to the mound and stood by Gabriel as they watched the kid trot to first. Duggan said, "Forget it."

"Yeah," said Gabriel.

"Way to go!" Andy said from the edge of the infield grass. "Excellent. Easy double play now!"

But the next kid hooked one through the infield right past him, and then Gabriel threw a curve that hung over the plate like a zeppelin and their clean-up hitter rocked it off the outfield wall.

The kid on first scored.

Duggan came out to the mound again.

"Get out of here," Gabriel told him.

Duggan shrugged, pulled his mask down and went back behind the plate. He didn't even signal for a pitch. Gabriel threw a fastball in the dirt.

"Hey, dirtball. Mudball!" taunted Pik.

"Concentrate!" Andy shouted.

Concentrate, thought Gabriel. Concentrate. He looked at Duggan. Now Duggan nodded, slightly. Gabriel narrowed the whole world down to the little channel of space between his hand and Duggan's mit. Concentrate.

He struck the next three kids out.

Tony Picarazzi, their right fielder, led off in the sixth. The Mantis got him out on a ground ball.

Robin Lenz, their second baseman, took a called third strike. Then Andy, with a full count, missed a slider that looked like a fastball.

Gabriel retaliated by getting the next three batters out, on a pop fly and two feeb dribblers, which he fielded and fired to first himself.

Gabriel led off in the seventh, swung at the Mantis's first pitch like some dumb rookie, and popped to third.

Then he had to sit on the bench and watch Ray take hold of one and drive it to the warning track before the center fielder backhanded it against the wall, for the second out.

And then Duggan singled, and Pik lined out.

Half an inning later, Johnson was at bat again. The Mantis was sweating. Gabriel, watching him pitch, hoped his arm would fall off.

But it didn't. Not in time to save MacDonald, Wright, and Picarazzi. Gabriel picked up his glove, disgustedly.

"What I'm thinking," Coach said, "is maybe you should come out, Gabriel. Let someone else pitch."

"Are you kidding?" Gabriel couldn't believe it.

"Leave him in!" Pik stepped next to Gabriel.

"What're you, giving the orders?" asked Coach.

"You'll blow the *game*," said Pik.

"Hey," said Ray. "Our turn."

Coach let it go. They took the field. Gabriel

assumed from Coach's silence that they'd won the argument. He was glad, but he felt bad at the same time. Still, if Coach really wanted to be in charge, he should do something, Gabriel argued with himself.

He forgot to concentrate. Flood's first batter took one of Gabriel's curves deep to the fence in left center, but Ray ran it down. He struck the next two kids out, but they both took him to a full count. Now *he* was sweating.

The seventh inning went by — three up, three down; three up, three down — and they'd see-sawed into the eighth.

Andy was the leadoff batter. He missed two quick strikes.

"C'mon Andy. You can do it," said Gabriel.

Pik said, "I'll break this bat over my head if we lose."

"Promises, promises," Duggan said.

Andy got wood on the next pitch and singled into the right-field gap, motored around first, and tried to grab the extra base.

The Flood left fielder, caught flat-footed, waited just a moment too long to make the throw. Andy slid into second headfirst and beat the tag.

"*Awwwwright!*" screamed Gabriel, while the bench broke out in cheers around him.

He picked up his bat, and headed for the batter's box.

C'mon, insect, he said to himself. C'mon, Mantis, bring it. Bring it and see what happens.

The Mantis brought it and Gabriel topped it. He ran anyway, screaming in frustration, only to find he'd beaten the throw to first. He was safe. The ball had taken a bad bounce and the shortstop had fumbled it.

Andy would have made that play, thought Gabriel. The Flood first baseman wouldn't look at him.

Ray was up. Please, thought Gabriel. Let it be Ray and not Duggan who's the hero. Let it be Ray.

The Mantis hung a curve. Gabriel saw it, Andy saw it, Ray saw it. Everyone saw it. Andy gave a little hop of anticipation on second base as Ray did what he always said you were supposed to do to a hanging curve — make it a frozen rope.

The ball screamed off his bat at about a thousand miles an hour, and about nine feet above the field. It looked sure to clear the fence.

Andy rounded third and sprinted for home.

The Flood center fielder leaped up. The tip of his glove went back. He went back.

He came down holding Ray's frozen rope in an ice-cream cone catch.

"Go back!" screamed Gabriel to Andy. "Go back!"

Andy made it back as far as third.

The double play ended the inning.

Gabriel held them in the top of the ninth. So what, he thought, heading for the bench.

When Duggan popped up, Gabriel didn't even care.

Everyone was quiet as he came back to the dugout. The silence continued as Pik flied out.

That left Mike MacDonald. They watched him without hope. Mike fouled off the third strike, twice.

"Please," said Pik.

Mike singled to right.

Then Steve Wright came up and singled off the third baseman's glove.

"Whoa," said Andy. "Look at that! All right! All right, let's go!"

Tony Picarazzi fouled off seven pitches, waited out three straight balls, and then walked. The bases were loaded.

Now the bench really woke up. No one could hear himself scream, they were all shouting so hard. Robin Lenz walked up to the plate.

The Mantis threw a dirtball.

Then another.

"No way," shouted Pik joyfully.

Was the Mantis actually going to walk their number-nine hitter?

The manic noise in the dugout got louder.

Too loud. Gabriel noticed with a faint twinge of

apprehension that Coach had unhooked one of his earphones. Now he was signalling Robin. Lenz nodded. MacDonald, on third, looked fairly puzzled. Coach signalled again. MacDonald nodded.

Gabriel shook his head violently. "Coach!"

Andy'd caught on, too. "Hey, Coach?"

Pik turned. "What're you guys . . . ?"

The Mantis let fly, MacDonald broke from third, and Lenz squared around to bunt.

Pik screamed, Andy looked away, Gabriel closed his eyes.

Lenz missed the ball. MacDonald was tagged out.

The game was over.

"Are you *nuts*?" Pik shouted as Lenz, Picarazzi, and MacDonald walked miserably toward the dugout. His words lashed through the defeated silence. Coach's face got red.

"Pik," said Andy, trying to calm him down.

"You crazy? You call a suicide squeeze in that situation? All we had to do was *wait*. Their pitcher was gonna walk him. *Walk* him."

"Pik." Gabriel said.

"Sometimes you try things," Coach said. "We're here to have fun. You got a problem with fun, Telander?"

"What I have a problem with is idiot coaching," Pik muttered.

"That's *enough*, Telander. Now, get out there and behave like good sports."

They lined up. They walked past the Flood team, swiping at each other's hands, muttering, "Good game. Congratulations."

They sat back down in the dugout, Andy, Ray, Pik, and Gabriel, watching the winning team leave the field. They each felt responsible for the loss.

"I hate this game," said Pik.

"It wasn't any one thing," Andy said. "It should never have come down to one thing. If I hadn't caused that double play earlier, heading for home like that. . . ."

"You want to take all the credit for losing? Forget it." Gabriel looked at both of them. "You think we played *good*? It shouldn't've happened that way."

Pik looked in the direction of Coach's car, turning out of the parking lot. "Eat dirt and die. This is as bad as we've ever played. Ever."

No one answered. They'd lost to Flood. There wasn't anything else to say.

4.
Who's on First?

The evening sky was deep purple, almost black. Gabriel and Andy and Ray rode their bikes past lines of parked cars, past fenced-in yards, and, not far from Pik's house, past a group of little kids playing stickball under a streetlight. The night was warm and they could smell hamburgers and chicken cooking on backyard grills — a summer smell, even though summer was still a few weeks away and school wasn't out yet.

When they got to Pik's, they stowed their bikes on the back porch and knocked on the door. Pik's mom let them in and sent them upstairs to Pik's room, where they found him lying on his bed, wearing blue sweatpants and a Michael Jordan T-shirt, flipping a baseball in the air and catching it, over and over, up and down. He hardly looked at them when they came in.

" 'S up?" Gabriel said.

"You guys drop in on everybody without calling first?" Pik asked.

"No, just on mental patients," said Andy.

Pik glanced at him, but kept flipping the base-ball. "Don't go into comedy," he advised Andy. "You'll starve."

Andy faked a charge, but Pik just lay there, flipping the baseball, up and down, up and down.

Gabriel and Ray sauntered over to the bookcase and began looking at the books: airplanes, ships, tanks, weapons. There were also books on ani-mals, especially reptiles.

Andy stood in the middle of the room, staring at the big terrarium, with its bright, warm light shining down on Heinrich. Andy shook his head. "That is one ugly dude," he said.

"Watch your mouth," Pik said. "Iguanas have feelings."

"Aw, Hair," Andy cooed. "I didn't mean it. You're such a pretty boy." Hair was short for The Hairless Wonder, Andy's nickname for Heinrich. He went over and looked down at Heinrich. "How you been, old buddy?" He reached into the ter-rarium and picked him up. "How's the grossest creature on earth?"

On the bed, Pik stopped flipping the baseball.

The iguana sat on Andy's arm, not even moving his tail.

"Entertaining," Andy said, shaking his head. "Real interesting." He pretended to drop-kick him, then placed him gently back on the warm rocks of the terrarium.

Pik sat up and swiveled around. He grabbed a jacket and a baseball cap off the floor, threw them into his closet and slid the door shut. He looked at Gabriel and Ray and said, "Hang out here a minute," then ducked out of the room.

Gabriel and Andy and Ray exchanged looks.

"He's still sore about losing last week," said Gabriel.

Andy answered, "He can be such a dweeb at times." He picked up an old Rubik's cube from Pik's desk and flopped down on the bed, his shoulders against the wall, his feet hanging off the edge.

Gabriel pulled a couple of books off the bookshelf and peered at them. He wanted to soften Pik up, get him to laugh, be himself. He hated it when Pik and Andy fought — there was nothing he could do to stop it, and it could go on for a long time, ruining everything.

He looked at the books in his hands. They were about the Civil War. He put them back and pulled out a couple more.

Down the hall, a toilet flushed. A moment later, Pik entered the room, dodging an ME 109 that hung from the ceiling. He went over and straddled the desk chair, his back to the desk. He looked at Ray. "So what are we doing tonight?"

Holding a book, Gabriel turned and looked at Pik. "Watch some tube?" he asked. "I don't know, what are you up for?"

Pik didn't look at Gabriel or Andy. "I wonder what Coach would want us to do. Squeeze play? Or just sit on our butts?"

Andy said, "Whatever he wanted, you'd do the opposite, right?"

"Come on you guys," Gabriel said.

"So what are we doing?" Pik asked.

"Actually," said Gabriel, "there's a film on later I thought you guys might like."

"A film?" asked Pik.

"Yeah. *Abbott and Costello Meet Frankenstein.*"

"That's a *film*?"

"Yeah, it's a film. What do you think it is?"

"A *movie*. Not a *film*."

Gabriel laughed. "Whatever." He slid a book back on the shelf and pulled out another.

"A *film*," Pik said.

Andy said, "What channel?"

"Cable," said Gabriel.

Pik shook his head. "You couldn't have mentioned this earlier?" All four of them knew that Pik didn't have cable.

Ray said to Gabriel, "Why don't we go over to your house?"

"My parents are having people over."

"They gonna be watching TV?" said Pik.

"They'll probably be in the living room."

There was a silence. Andy worked the Rubik's cube.

Gabriel turned back to the bookshelf, pulled another book out, flipped through it.

Andy twisted the multicolored cube, his hands and wrists flying. Suddenly, he tossed the cube onto the bed — solved, each side a solid color — and said, "Okay, let's try my place. But I think my dad'll be home."

Pik got up and fussed with Heinrich's terrarium.

Gabriel said, "Hey, what's this?" He pulled a couple of shiny CDs out from behind some books.

Pik turned around. "Nothing," he said. "CDs."

"I can see that." They had no covers. Gabriel examined them. "Bobby Brown," he read aloud. "Guns N' Roses. Bon Jovi."

Andy looked up. "What are you doing with CDs?"

"Yeah," Ray said, looking at Pik. "You don't have a CD player."

Pik stretched. "I'm saving up for one. I started my collection early. Is that all right with you guys?"

"Where're the covers to these?" Gabriel asked.

Pik said, "What is this, the KGB? Put those back." He walked out of the room.

Gabriel and Andy stared after him, then finally looked at one another.

"*Starting a collection?*" Gabriel asked.

"*Saving up?*" echoed Andy.

Downstairs, Pik's father was sitting in the living room, watching TV, a can of A&W root beer on the floor by the chair. The rest of the house was dark and quiet.

Pik went over and stood beside the TV. "Hey Dad," he said, "I'm going over to Andy's."

His father reached out, picked up the remote control, and zapped off the sound. He shifted in his big chair, gave a sigh. "Sure, why not?" He looked around and saw Ray and Andy and Gabriel standing by the door. "Hey, how you doin'? Come in." He gestured with the remote toward the chairs opposite the couch.

Pik said, "We were just taking off. We're going to catch a movie on cable. Excuse me, a film."

"Right," said Mr. Telander. "Don't stay out too late. A *film*?"

"I won't."

They rode their bikes through the dark to Andy's. The back door was unlocked. In the kitchen, Pik opened the fridge and checked out the contents. He grabbed half a sandwich, unwrapped it, and stuffed it into his mouth.

Five seconds later he was spitting it into the waste can in the corner.

"Sardines," Andy said, laughing.

Gabriel tried not to.

Andy said, "I'll go find my Dad."

Gabriel and Ray sat down at the kitchen table. Pik stood over the sink, like he was going to heave.

"Ever see this?" Gabriel asked. *Abbott and Costello Meet Frankenstein.*"

Pik shook his head.

"It's really funny," Gabriel said. "I hope he lets us watch it."

Andy's dad was pretty strict. Andy's mother didn't live at home; she'd left his father a long time ago, and Andy had told them that he hardly remembered her. His dad, a doctor, seemed to work every minute of every day, and when Dr. Kim was at home working in his study, he didn't tolerate any noise in the house.

Pik was scowling, picking at his teeth with his tongue.

"Sardine bones?" said Gabriel.

"I was thinking, ham and cheese," said Pik. "I was thinking, bologna."

Gabriel said, "Hey look, I've been thinking about that game."

"Forget it," Pik said.

"No, really," Gabriel insisted.

"I'm fed up," Pik said. "I'm not really mad at Andy, I guess. I'm just mad, in general. I mean, losing to Flood is bad enough, but when your own coach beats you. . . ." He looked disgusted and angry.

"I know," Gabriel said. "But you can't let it bother you."

"I know what's bothering *you*," Pik said. "You're all hung up on Duggan. You probably thought as much about Duggan in that game as you did about Flood. No wonder you pitched like a stiff. Forget about Duggan. Just let him alone. He's a gamer. He's okay."

"Who said anything about Duggan?" asked Gabriel, annoyed that Pik would catch on.

"He's just got a mind of his own," Ray said.

"He's gettin' good," Gabriel said. "No doubt about it. I'm glad about that."

"Right," Pik said. "We could use more guys like him. I doubt the four of us can carry this crew all season."

Gabriel snorted. "Apparently not."

"We've got to forget that game," said Pik. "Put it out of our minds. Concentrate on the next one."

"Against Flood?"

"Do we *play* Flood next?"

"No — Milford."

"Well then," said Pik, "that's the game you

oughta be thinking about. Milford."

Gabriel almost made some crack, but realized Pik was right. What was the use of thinking about Flood? The immediate challenge was the game against Milford, just a few days off.

They heard a door close, and Andy came in. He opened the fridge. "Anybody want anything?"

"Got a sandwich?" asked Gabriel. "Something *fishy*?"

Pik said, "So what's the deal? We staying, or what?"

Andy closed the refrigerator door and put his hands in his jeans pockets. "Dad says he's in the middle of something. He says it's important. He says he'd rather I didn't have the TV on."

Gabriel looked from Ray to Pik. He raised his eyebrows.

Ray drummed his fingers on the counter.

"Yo, Gabe," Pik said.

"My turn," Gabriel said. "Let us check out the agenda at the Fixx abode."

They headed out the back door.

At Gabriel's house, the small kitchen was bright and noisy and crowded. Six adults sat around the kitchen table, playing cards. Duhe got up off the floor and came over to Gabriel, whipping his big tail against the kitchen cabinets.

Gabriel's father stopped the game for a moment

and introduced the boys to the adults. After everybody said hello to everybody else, Gabriel said they were going to watch television.

"Sure," said his father. "Go for it."

The adults laughed.

The boys and Duhe hurried into the living room. Gabriel turned on the tube and fiddled with the VCR. He decided to tape the movie as they watched it. The movie had already begun. It was in black and white. A man's face filled the screen, his eyes wide with fear. He kept trying to point out an opening coffin lid, but he stuttered too much and couldn't speak.

"Which one's the fat guy?" Andy said.

"That's Abbott," Pik said.

"No, that's Costello," Gabriel said.

The tall, thin one was running around frantically. "Is that Lou, or Bud?" said Pik. "Is that Lou Abbott, or Bud Costello?"

"Bud Abbott. Lou Costello."

"Bud's the fat one?" Ray asked.

"Yeah. Now shut up."

"Did you guys ever see 'Who's on first?' " said Andy.

"What?"

"No, he's on second."

"Come *on*."

"What?"

"You know, the baseball routine," Andy said.

"See, the names of the players are things like Who, What, and I Don't Know."

"Didn't we see that a couple . . . yeah," said Pik. "We saw that."

"Hey," said Andy, "is that Frankenstein?"

"That's Dracula," said Gabriel. "If you'd pay attention . . . you know, 'Frankenstein' is really the doctor's name, the guy who made him."

"You mean, the big guy with the bolts in his neck isn't Frankenstein?"

"Well, in this movie he is, but in the original, it's — "

"I though this was a *film*," Pik said.

"What?"

"Frankenstein."

"He's the shortstop," Ray said.

"Uh, guys?" Gabriel said. "I'm not getting much out of this film — movie — here. You know?"

"You Know's on third."

"Gag me."

"Gag *him*."

For a few moments, they watched the movie in silence. After a while, Pik, who was looking entirely bored, rolled over and started pulling the hairs between the pads of Duhe's feet. Duhe growled, moved his hind leg, reached back and licked the bottom of his foot.

"Do dogs see black and white movies in color?" Pik asked.

47

Gabriel threw a pillow at him.

"You taping this?" Andy said.

"Yeah."

"Then let's play some football," said Andy. He juggled the pillow Gabriel had thrown at Pik. "Me and you, Pik and Ray."

Gabriel said, "Now you're talking."

"We're gonna whip your butts," Pik said.

Duhe stood up and growled, tail thumping against the couch. Andy and Gabriel slapped five.

So upstairs in Gabriel's room it was pillow football, and for a while it was all even, with the furniture getting the worst of it; but then the game got rougher, and noisier. Cries were heard all the way downstairs in the kitchen where the adults paused in their poker game, listening to what sounded like thunder.

Upstairs, Andy and Pik were on the floor, laughing uncontrollably. Ray was sitting on Andy's head; Duhe was standing in the middle of the room barking at the feathers that swirled everywhere like snow; Gabriel was lying on the bed holding his stomach, laughing and spitting feathers out of his mouth — relieved because two of his best friends had practically killed each other and now seemed to be friends again.

5.
Winning Isn't Everything

As the four of them walked toward the Milford Junior High diamond, Gabriel already had his game face on. It was a good day for baseball: breezy and clear; warm, but not too hot. Gabriel hardly noticed the weather, though, because he was thinking about the games against Milford, last summer. Both had been close. Johnson won the first, but Milford came from behind to steal the second. And Milford went on to take the runner-up spot in summer-league play, second to Flood. Johnson had wound up third.

Without saying much to anyone, Gabriel found Ronnie Duggan and began warming up. He kept an eye on the Milford players taking infield practice and shagging flies. They looked flashy in their home whites. The shortstop handled ground balls smoothly, and there was a tall outfielder who had good speed. But Gabriel was keeping an eye out for their catcher. He was worried about him. He remembered him as a big kid with dirty hair sticking out from the back of his cap, very tough to get out. Had a late swing that looked like he'd never get around on it, then BOOM! — three-run dinger to the opposite field.

Ray and Pik were playing catch with Andy. Pik said, as if he were reading Gabriel's mind, "Where's Godzilla? From last year, you know? With the hair."

"No sign of him," Gabriel said.

Milford had two pitchers warming up, neither of them very big, and as Gabriel watched, one of them kept throwing the ball past the catcher. Either the kid couldn't throw strikes, or the catcher couldn't catch. The dirty-haired catcher didn't seem to be around.

Excellent, Gabriel thought. He bore down and threw a blistering fastball to Duggan.

Andy led off the game by walking. On the first pitch to Gabriel, he stole second. Gabriel took a couple more pitches, then hit a sharp liner up the middle that the pitcher waved at feebly. Andy broke for third, but the shortstop came out of nowhere and lunged as the ball sailed toward the outfield. It snagged in the kid's glove, way up in the webbing: a snow cone. He scrambled to his feet and stepped on second, doubling up Andy.

Two outs, just like that.

Ray swung at the first pitch, hitting a blooper,

foul. The third baseman caught it easily.

Three up, three down.

Gabriel felt uncomfortable on the mound, throwing his warm-up pitches. Couldn't get his balance; wasn't following through. He hated pitching on diamonds away from home — the mounds were never the same. Also, he was stewing about the double play. They'd blown a great opportunity. And who else on the team was going to score runs, if the four of them didn't? A bad first inning could set the tempo of a whole game.

He finished his warm-ups and Ronnie Duggan fired the ball to Andy at second. Duggan had a good arm, he had to admit it. He caught the ball from MacDonald, at third, and turned to face the lead-off batter.

It was obvious, after two pitches, that the kid was looking for a walk. Gabriel's first pitch had been close, his second right down the middle — both fastballs — and the kid hadn't so much as moved his bat. Gabriel stepped off the rubber and considered his options. He decided to test his theory. He stepped back on the rubber, wound up, and threw a slow fastball over the heart of the plate, waist high.

The kid clobbered it toward the gap in left center. Ray raced over and cut it off. He fired it into Andy, who relayed it to second, holding the kid to a single.

You total moron, Gabriel said to himself. *Total moron!* Wake up and get in the game.

He walked the next batter.

Pik sauntered over to the mound. "Pick this guy off," he said to Gabriel. "Second pitch." He clunked Gabriel on the shoulder with his big mitt and walked back to first.

Gabriel went into his stretch, checked the runner at second, and made a point of ignoring the runner at first. He knew Pik would be playing off the bag. He threw a curve, outside, for ball one.

Next pitch. Stretch. Check the runner at second. Whirl and fire to first.

Pik glided in behind the runner, caught the ball and tagged the kid on the arm as he dived back toward the bag.

"Out!" the umpire hollered.

Yo, Gabriel thought. Excellent!

Man on second, one out.

The next batter looked vaguely familiar, Gabriel wasn't sure why. He had long red hair and freckles, and oddly stood way forward in the batter's box. A right-hander, he reached for an outside pitch and lashed it between Pik and the second baseman. Tony Picarazzi, in right, was playing shallow and got the ball in quickly to Pik, holding the lead runner at third.

First and third, one out, and the number-four batter coming to the plate. This guy Gabriel remembered: he was the tall left-hander who played center field, the kid Gabriel'd noticed warming up. Sometimes he pitched. He hit for average, and every now and then he crushed one.

Gabriel thought, well, I'll pitch to the guy, and we'll just see.

But the home plate umpire called time. Coach Morris was heading toward the mound.

Pik and Andy trotted over, and Ronnie Duggan hustled out from his position at home.

"What do you think, boys?" Coach said. He shoved his Red Sox cap back on his head. "Intentional walk? We might have a better shot at getting the next guy."

"Now you're thinking," Pik said.

"I like it, Coach," said Andy.

Coach nodded. "Gabe?"

Great, thought Gabriel, just as I'm getting my rhythm. But he nodded.

"I'll go along with that," he said.

"Okay," Coach said. "Be careful with the walk. Keep it outside, but don't throw it away. Next hitter comes up, Andy, play everybody in close. Look for a force at home, maybe a double play. Keep the ball low, Gabe — go for a ground ball. Got it?"

The conference ended, and Gabriel walked the left-hander, intentionally.

Bases loaded, one out. Infield in.

Gabriel's first pitch to the next kid was a fast-ball, low. Too low. The ball bounced in the dirt in front of home plate. It squirted away from Duggan, who threw his mask high in the air and scampered after it. Gabriel dashed toward the plate as the runners took off. The ball hit the bottom of the screen and popped upward; Duggan picked it out of the air like an apple from a tree. He turned and threw perfectly to Gabriel, who slapped a tag on the sliding Milford player.

Out number two. Runners on second and third.

"Nothing too good," Coach called from the bench, afterward, like nothing had happened. "First base is open."

With the count 2-and-2, the batter hit a looping line drive toward left field. Andy chased it, leaped, and snared it backhanded. Great play!

End of the first.

Gabriel felt as though he'd been run over. Yet they'd somehow kept Milford from scoring.

"Still tied!" he said to Pik, on the bench.

"Miracle." Pik looked at him glumly. "We oughta be up by four or five."

It was a strange game. Johnson would look hapless one minute, great the next. Then things got stranger.

Gabriel couldn't get Milford's number-three and number-four hitters out. He remembered the red-haired kid, finally — remembered him from the summer before. The guy would do anything to get on base: hit to the opposite field, bunt, crowd the plate and take a pitch in the arm. The guy batting clean-up was just a good hitter: he'd hit the ball hard every time. Usually it'd fall in for a single or a double, and the red-haired kid would chug around the bases in front of him.

But as it became clear that those two were the only decent hitters on the team, Gabriel began to settle down: good fastball, good curve, throwing mostly strikes, dispatching each batter on just a few pitches. He was feeling good, feeling strong, and there wasn't a chance that he'd get tired.

Meanwhile, his guys were finally showing signs that they knew what a baseball bat was made for.

In the second inning, they scratched out a run on a walk, a good bunt, an error by the second baseman, and a passed ball.

In the third, they blew it open: A pop-up behind second that dropped in started it, followed by a full-swing bunt. The ball hit the plate, bounced erratically toward short, and rolled to a stop — just out of reach of the pitcher and the third baseman.

So when Andy came to the plate, there were two on and nobody out. He watched a couple of pitches go by, then laced the ball between the shortstop and the third baseman. That drove in a run, and when the throw went all the way home, Andy motored into second with ease.

Second and third, no outs.

Gabriel stepped up and singled, driving in two more.

Ray singled; Gabriel advanced to second.

And then Duggan stepped to the plate. He hit a line drive way out in the gap between center and left, and because there was no fence, the ball just kept rolling. Duggan made it home, standing up.

Johnson had scored six runs in their half of the third, all before Milford got an out. It put the good guys ahead, 7–0.

As the game continued, things kept swinging Johnson's way. They scored one more in the fourth, three in the fifth, one in the sixth, and two more in the eighth. Gabriel was overpowering the Milford hitters, except for the red-haired kid and the clean-up hitter. Let 'em go, he thought. Nobody'll drive 'em in.

Johnson went into the top of the ninth leading 14–0.

Gabriel sat on the bench with Andy and Pik and watched Milford's pitcher walk Robin Lenz, their number-nine hitter.

"Oops," said Pik. He was laughing. Andy didn't say anything. He looked like he was feeling sorry for the kid. Gabriel wasn't sure how he felt, but he knew he'd hate to be in that spot: losing 14–0 and unable to get the ball over the plate. Then Milford's pitcher walked Andy and Gabriel.

Ray batted with the bases loaded, and the kid actually threw him a strike. Ray rewarded him by doubling, clearing the bases.

Duggan drove one deep; the Milford right fielder made a desperate running catch, and fell down. Ray took off from second like Rickey Henderson, ran through Coach Morris's stop sign at third, and scored well ahead of the relay.

"Hey DeVellis!" Coach yelled. "Watch for my *sign!*"

Pik stepped to the plate and singled on the 3–0 pitch.

Coach Morris threw his Red Sox cap on the ground. "I gave you the *take* sign!" he yelled at Pik.

The first pitch to Mike MacDonald was way outside. Pik broke for second; the catcher was so amazed he didn't even throw, and Pik went in standing up. He danced off the base, mocking the pitcher.

Coach Morris asked for time, and walked out to Pik at second.

Pik watched him.

"What do you think you're doing?" Coach asked.

"Stealing second, Coach. See? Here I am."

"Did I give you the steal sign?"

"They weren't expecting it," Pik laughed. "No throw."

Coach shook his head. "I'm not talking results here, I'm talking baseball. You're ahead 17, 18 runs. We don't need the extra base. You don't take a chance in that situation. You don't show up the other team. You don't disobey the 'take' sign. And you *don't* steal unless I tell you." He was holding his forefinger and thumb together, and jabbing at Pik.

"These guys couldn't throw out Heinrich," Pik said.

"That's not the . . . *Heinrich?*" said Coach, interrupting himself. "Who's Heinrich? Never mind, that's not the point. The point is, take a ride on the pine. You're benched."

"What?"

"You heard me. We're getting a pinch runner here." Coach Morris turned around and stalked back to the dugout.

When Gabriel saw Pik coming toward the bench with the Coach, he was afraid Pik'd gotten hurt. "What's the matter?" he asked him.

"Nothing!" Pik's face was red, and Gabriel thought he could hear little grinding noises from his jaw. "He took me out 'cause I stole second. Said we didn't need the extra base."

"Sit," Gabriel said, pulling him down by the arm. "Cool off."

Pik knocked Gabriel's hand away. "Come on, cream it!" he yelled at Steve Wright.

Gabriel watched as the pitcher threw two balls past the catcher, and the pinch runner went to third, then scored. That's the way to do it, Gabriel thought; you don't stop running, throwing, and hitting, just because you have a lead.

Steve Wright swung hard at the 2–0 pitch, which was low and would have been ball three, and hit a dribbler right at the pitcher. The kid picked it up and managed to throw a strike to the first baseman. Two outs. Tony Picarazzi walked toward the plate.

Pik stopped pacing and sat down between Andy and Gabriel. "You can hit this jerk!" he yelled at Tony.

"Hey." Andy shook his head. "We're trashing these guys. Why rub it in?"

"Look who's talking!" Pik said to Andy. "You took two bases after tagging up."

Andy shrugged. "Maybe I shouldn't have."

"If the base is there," Pik said, "you take it. I don't care what the score is."

Gabriel said, "What if the score's reversed? What if we're losing 18–0? You gonna steal a base then?"

"Heck yeah," Pik said. "That pitcher has a slow delivery, the catcher has a pasta arm. The crime would be *not* stealing."

59

Andy shook his head. "I don't know, Pik. There's gotta be a difference between winning and humiliating guys."

"Name it," said Pik.

That seemed to end the argument.

They won the game.

Afterward, walking toward the waiting cars, Gabriel said, "How 'bout Coach? 'Take it easy, don't take it easy.' 'Don't play hard, get these guys out.' "

"Adults, man," Andy said. "Weird."

"I know two things," Pik said. "We won. We dominated."

Andy grinned. "Isn't it fun?"

"Yeah," said Gabriel.

"As long as we keep winning," said Pik.

They stopped walking and looked at one another.

"As long as we win the rest," Pik said. "All of 'em."

Gabriel nodded.

"So what're we doing tomorrow?" Andy asked.

"Let's do something in the morning," Gabriel said.

"The mall," Pik said. "We'll get something to eat."

Gabriel said, "Me, I'm gonna send a scorecard to that red-haired kid."

"Or the catcher with the hair," Andy added. "Godzilla, who didn't show up."

	1	2	3	4	5	6	7	8	9	R	H	E
JOHNSON	0	1	6	1	3	1	0	2	8	22	25	2
MILFORD	0	0	0	0	0	0	0	0	3	3	7	9

Gabriel hit the mall early. Locking his bike outside, he noticed Pik's, but didn't see Ray's or Andy's. He wandered around for a while, keeping an eye out for Pik. The mall was like an air-conditioned city. In the discount sporting-goods store, he checked out baseball spikes and Franklin batting gloves. Both his spikes and his batting glove were wearing out. He had fifteen dollars on him, but it wasn't enough for spikes, and no way was he going to spend it all on a batting glove.

He wandered into Borders Bookstore and flipped through some posters — there was a new one of Wade Boggs, batting, and one of Kevin Mitchell, catching a fly ball bare-handed.

He wandered out of there and into Recordland. The place had mirrors on three walls and Madonna playing from about sixteen speakers. He only bought cassette tapes, but he liked looking at the covers of record albums. He walked down the rack and found Skid Row. Man, the chain that guy wore, he thought. Ear to nose.

He wondered how he'd look with an earring . . . maybe just a little one.

There was a mirror on the wall in front of him; he looked up to check out his ear and nose, imagining a chain connecting the two, when the weirdest thing happened: in the mirror he saw Pik, behind him. He was about to turn around and say something when he saw Pik pull a CD out of a rack. He froze, but he wasn't sure why. Pik glanced toward the front counter and quickly stripped off the packaging. He slipped the shiny CD under his T-shirt and tucked his shirt tail into his jeans. Then he turned and walked slowly out of the store.

Gabriel leaned on the record rack for a moment, thinking. Had he really just seen that?

No doubt about it.

He walked out of Recordland, looking up and down the mall's main drag.

Pik was nowhere in sight.

He wasn't sure what to do.

He shook his head. *Pik? Shoplifting?*

It was bizarre. It was funny, too, somehow — funny-strange: Pik, of all people.

He laughed out loud.

Shoppers stared at him. People gave him plenty of clearance. But he was concerned about Pik.

They were friends. And he didn't think that friends kept anything like that from each other.

On the way out of the mall, he considered telling Andy.

Then he wondered if Andy already knew.

6.
The Mantis

They were itching to get at Flood. They were dying to get at Flood. Steamrolling Milford, they topped that with another crusher over a team from Lakeside. Victory after victory followed until their record was 11—1. Still, nothing meant anything, except evening the score with Flood, which was 12–0.

The night before the game, Gabriel lay in bed, visualizing his game: where he was going to hit, what he was going to pitch, all of it — the way he'd read that George Brett did, the night before games.

Andy watched a little TV, turned down low so his father wouldn't get on his case. He didn't mention the game, his father didn't ask. Better that way. He tried to think of other things while he was falling asleep.

Pik watched Heinrich. Heinrich stared back and won; Pik blinked first. He rolled over, staring into the darkness, listening to the TV loud and clear from the living room, where his parents sat bathed in its light — silent even when the laugh tracks rolled by.

Their field. Their home game.

Too bad, thought Gabriel, walking onto the field the next morning. Too bad it was just summer league, with a summer-league crowd: parents, kids who were bored, girls with crushes. Still, it gave Johnson an edge. Had to. Gabriel grinned. No way Johnson's home field was raked dirt and smooth velvet grass, like at Flood. No way Flood was used to these kinds of conditions. Warming up, feeling the hot sun beating down, knowing all the pits and craters and soft spots on the field, Gabriel felt a sudden affection for it.

The four of them were forty minutes early, the first players from Johnson to show up. Flood had already started warming up. The whole team, smooth, new, spotless.

"Glow in the dark, huh?" he said to Pik, nodding toward Flood.

"We can change that," said Pik.

"No problem," said Andy.

But it was, right from the start. Coach started Johnson with the same lineup they'd had when they'd played Flood before: Andy at short, Gabriel pitching, Ray in left, Ronnie Duggan catching, Pik at first, MacDonald on third, Wright in center, Picarazzi in right, Lenz on second. He reeled off the starters, then barked, "Any questions?"

As usual, Pik's hand went up.

Coach sighed, rolled his eyes. "What, Pik."

"That's *it*, Coach? That's all you've got to say?"

"That's it, Pik. That's my Whitey Herzog bit for the day."

"Coach," said Pik.

"Telander," Coach answered, "just for you: get out there, play ball, try to win. Okay?"

"But — "

"Okay, Telander?"

"I don't believe this," said Pik.

"Johnson coach? You ready?" called the umpire. They took the field.

Gabriel walked the first two batters. Hot day, he thought, but I'm not so hot. Shake it off, Fixx. He took a deep breath and blew three fastballs by their number-three hitter.

Andy's voice came over his shoulder. "Yo!"

Their clean-up hitter laid down a perfect bunt. MacDonald handled it okay, a solid throw from third. But he really didn't have a play. Bases loaded.

This is not good, thought Gabriel. He looked down at the ball; then at the number-five hitter. This is ridiculous, he thought. Then without thinking, he reared back and let fly at the guy's head.

The guy went down like he was shot.

Jeers and catcalls and cries of "Whoa, Studley!"

came from the Flood bench. Flood's coach, a blond guy with tennis-player arms and an island-resort tan, started jumping up and down, shouting, "Hey! Hey, ump!"

Hey, ump!" mimicked Pik.

The umpire called time and came out to the mound.

"That get away from you, son?" he asked.

"Yes, it did, sir." Gabriel looked him squarely in the eye. "I'm pretty embarrassed. It was supposed to be a curve."

The umpire held Gabriel's gaze a moment longer, then said, "Play ball, son. You get embarrassed again, you're out of the game."

Duggan called for a curve this time. Gabriel nodded, and shot one in, low and away. The kid lined it over Andy's head.

Score, 2–0.

Duggan pushed back his mask and stood up, like he was about to come out and talk to Gabriel. Gabriel put his hands on his hips, daring him. After a moment, Duggan squatted back down.

A kid who looked about two feet tall, someone Gabriel had never seen before, came out. His strike zone must have been about six inches. Whatever it was, Gabriel missed it, and the shrimp got a base on balls.

By the time Gabriel struck out the eighth hitter on three blazing fastballs for the third out, the score was 3–0. Gabriel was sweating.

Flood put in the same lineup as before, too, except for the shrimp, who was in right field. Figures, thought Gabriel, squinting through the glare.

Johnson flailed through the next three innings without touching the score, leaving people stranded on base at the end of each inning. *Flood victims.*

I hate this, thought Gabriel, coming up to the mound at the top of the fifth. From the looks on all the other faces, he wasn't alone. And now the Mantis was warming up.

Gabriel walked the shrimp again. Then, with two strikes on the next batter, he threw a curve that broke right past Duggan to the backstop, and the shrimp took second.

"Get a grip, Gabe!"

"Thanks," muttered Gabriel. "Thank a lot, Pik."

But it must have worked. He struck the batter out on the next three pitches. The next player followed with a bunt that Gabriel fielded himself. He took the shrimp out at third. The next guy popped out.

Gabriel was really sweating now. Everyone was. They were sweating, but they weren't playing.

"C'mon guys. Let's have some talk. Let's have some chatter!" Gabriel flopped down in the dugout as the Mantis walked out to the mound and took his warm-up pitches.

"Go team. Yea, team," muttered Duggan. He wasn't even bothering to unstrap his chest guard.

Andy didn't say anything. He just picked up his bat, walked out to the plate, and faced the Mantis like the kid had killed his whole family. He jumped on the second pitch and put it down into the left-field corner for a stand-up double.

"Yea *team*!" screamed Pik.

"Awright," said Ray softly.

Andy put his hands on his hips, grinning.

Gabriel was up next. The Mantis's first pitch broke down, just out of the strike zone. Nasty. He fired a fastball next, a little too close; Gabriel swung anyway — self-defense — and got a piece, just enough to tip it back over the catcher's head.

The Mantis stopped and stared. Gabriel stared back. *He's coming back with a fastball.* Gabriel knew it. He dug his feet in, windmilled the bat, and set himself.

Fastball.

Fastball, he kept thinking.

It was a fastball.

Gabriel swung.

Thwack! The ball went over the fence, still rising. It went so far, so fast, the center fielder didn't even bother to chase it.

The dugout went wild. They cheered Gabriel

around the bases — stood waiting for him as he crossed home; and he and Andy and Pik forearmed their high fives at home plate the way the Oakland A's did.

When the celebrating had died down, Ray grabbed his bat.

"Ray see, Ray do," he said. And he almost did. He doubled, and made it look easy.

And then Duggan singled him home.

Tie game, 3–3.

Now the Mantis was sweating. But he kept on, and got Pik out on a ground ball, MacDonald on a liner to third, and Wright on a long fly to deep center. The inning was over.

But Gabriel was in a groove now. He could feel it, winning was there, just waiting for him. All he had to do was . . . strike . . . each . . . player . . . out.

One, two, three, and Johnson was back at bat.

"Hey," complained Tony Picarazzi. "It's a long walk to right field. Give me some time. . . ."

They couldn't lose. They were loose, they were laughing.

The Mantis blew Picarazzi and Lenz away, and then got Andy on a long fly.

"All right," said Coach as they went back out on the field.

"I can't take much more of this," Pik growled.

"Of what?" said Andy, but Pik didn't say. Andy

didn't pursue it. This was the longest game he'd ever played. And the hottest. Flood. Water. Beaches . . . his mind started wandering, and he had to pull himself back. Pay attention, he told himself. Shortstop, remember. Top of the seventh, here, We're tied. We've got a chance.

Three up, three down; both teams.

"I've seen this movie before," complained Gabriel.

And then, suddenly, Johnson was ahead. In the bottom of the eighth, both Picarazzi and Lenz walked. Andy hit another screamer over the center fielder's head and off the base of the fence. He ended up on second — standing — with Picarazzi and Lenz scoring ahead of him.

"Yo, Gabriel!" shouted Picarazzi, and Gabriel swung at the first pitch and singled sharply to left. Andy scored, still standing.

As the Mantis wound up, Gabe thought, Hey, Mr. Mantis, watch this. He danced off the base. And then he decided to just do it.

He beat the throw. "Hey, hey, hey," he said, standing up, dusting himself off.

The bench went nuts.

Ray was up. Concentrating. Concentrating so hard his normal scowl was all smoothed out . . . his face blank. . . .

The Mantis fired 'em in. Strike. Ball. Fastball strike. Curve, too low . . . curve.

Ray swung at it and doubled it into the left-center gap. Gabriel rounded third at top speed, then walked home. And the center fielder fell for it. He threw the ball at the Flood catcher. Gabriel dove under it for the umpire's "Safe!" and Ray seized the chance to slide into third.

"Nice work," said Duggan, passing Gabriel on his way to the batter's box. Then he doubled Ray in.

Next, Pik slammed one into the Mantis's shin and before anyone knew it, Ray had scored.

"Incredible," said Gabriel, and he meant it. For the first time, Duggan really looked at Gabriel. Is he gonna smile? wondered Gabriel.

Duggan shrugged.

And then it was over. MacDonald flied out. Wright hit a rocket right at the first baseman, who stepped on the bag and got Pik for the inning-ending double play.

Andy handed Gabriel his glove, but suddenly Coach unplugged his Walkman.

"I think that's it for you today, Sport."

Andy stopped, but Coach waved him away. To Gabriel he said, "I'm gonna have Picarazzi relieve you."

"*Him*? No. Don't do it. Those guys'll *bury* him."

"Nobody's burying anybody. I feel bad I didn't give him work last game."

"That was then, this is now, Coach. This is Flood!"

Coach frowned at Gabriel. "What this is not, is a discussion, Fixx. We have a five run lead. Tony's pitching. You're in right."

"What's going on?"

Gabriel didn't stop to answer Pik, who was standing on first. Pik had eyes. He could see.

Sure enough, a minute later, he heard Pik. Nothing verbal. Just a lot of huffing and grunting and snorting, like a mad bull. A very mad bull.

Gabriel faced the infield and waited, talking to himself, as if he and Pik were doing a duet.

Tony wound up.

Flood's first batter singled. Tony walked the next kid.

Pik didn't even bother to keep his feelings quiet.

If Coach blows this game, Gabriel thought, I'll kill him. I'll kill him first. Before Pik gets to him.

The shrimp was up. I hate this little guy, thought Gabriel.

Tony struck him out.

Pik suddenly got quiet. Gabriel crouched. Maybe.

The next kid up was the lead-off batter. He lofted a ball right over Gabriel's head. Gabriel sprinted back, trying to keep his eye on it, dove

. . . and missed. Wright misplayed it off the fence and finally threw it in. An inside-park home run. Three runs scored.

Pik's bellow shattered the air, and what was left of Tony's confidence. Tony served up a tomato to the number-two hitter, who punched it over Steve Wright's head, for a double. The clean-up hitter delivered two massive fouls, and then another double. Their five-run lead was now a one-run lead.

"Tony." It was Ray, firm, calm. "You can do it."

Tony looked around wildly, wound and threw. Gabriel closed his eyes.

"*Striiike!*" called the umpire.

Pik was silent. The team was silent. Flood was going wild.

"Strike two!"

Gabriel opened his eyes.

The next pitch was a ball.

"Go Tony!" shouted Andy.

"Please, Tony," breathed Gabriel.

Another ball.

The whole game seemed to stop for one hot, airless moment. Gabriel was sweating, but he was shivering. The hottest part of the afternoon, the hottest part of the day. *"Pulllease."*

Tony wound up. He threw.

It was a frozen rope to end all frozen ropes.

Maybe that's why I was shivering, thought Gabriel, watching it rocket out of sight. I knew it was coming.

The batter trotted around the bases with his game-winning two-run homer. The hero.

They'd lost to Flood. Again.

7.
The Tournament

Already it was past mid-August. Summer was almost gone. Nearly every day, it seemed, window-rattling thunderstorms rumbled through Stratford and headed out across the Long Island Sound. The nights were cool. Kids who had gone away, came back. Practice started for the high school football team. Stores at the mall in Trumbull held back-to-school sales.

Early one morning, the week of the tournament, Gabriel lay stretched out on his bed, thinking it over.

What good was it?

What good was any of it, since they'd gone and lost to Flood? Twice.

The regular season had ended a few days before. Gabriel had no plans. School was right around the corner.

How depressing could it get?

A whole summer. A whole summer of baseball — and they lose to Flood twice. Twice! So they wind up second in the summer league.

What was the point, then?

Did it help that those two games with Flood were, in their own way, the best games he'd ever played in? Intense, well-played, close. Great competition.

No.

That was all consolation, second-place stuff. The way losers thought.

Winners didn't need consolation.

For coming out tops in the summer league, the Flood players all received individual trophies. The Johnson players got squat. You didn't get a trophy for second place.

Still, Gabriel could close his eyes and imagine it; remember a few key moments, visualize a few choice moves.

He thought of them as *mind-films*: The way Pik would stretch for an off-line throw from Andy . . . or the way Andy would leap for a drive over his head, then stomp around and raise dust with his spikes, mad at himself for not pulling down a ball even Michael Jordan couldn't have touched . . . or Ray in the outfield, seeing him turn and go back, straight toward the fence, and twist around at just the right moment, getting his glove high over his shoulder and pulling the ball down . . . or Pik apologizing to Coach Morris, half pretending, half not, saying he'd been outta line, but then grinning at Gabriel as he walked away . . . or that one stormy afternoon last spring, the four of them sliding on their bellies in the mud and the rain.

It was *that* stuff that made the game worth playing — and made it *almost* worth playing when they lost to Flood. But everything was *so* much sweeter — *would be* so much sweeter — if only they could beat Flood.

Well, the tournament was coming up: the end-of-season league tournament. Two days of baseball. If they won their first three games, then — the way they'd probably be seeded, with Flood first, Johnson second — they could meet Flood in the finals. It just might happen: to play Flood last, in the finals. It might happen — a chance to redeem themselves.

Out of nowhere, Gabriel started thinking about Pik. Not Pik playing baseball, but Pik stealing CDs. He'd pushed it to the back of his mind all summer long. He'd almost convinced himself that it wasn't real. But it was.

What was going on with Pik? What'd he have to go and do that for?

Gabriel hated to think about it. Because when he did, he also thought that he might have to tell somebody about it.

Lying there on his bed, he sighed. His mind drifted back to baseball. At least the season had ended on a high note — an 18–1 laugher over Nichols. He had pitched three innings, then played third while Mike MacDonald pitched. Coach wanted to give MacDonald some work because they'd need him to pitch during the tournament. Gabriel had seen Andy holding his breath when Coach announced the move, but this had been different from the Flood game: they were already up 13–0, and Nichols had no hitters anyway; even so, Gabriel hadn't given Coach the satisfaction of letting him know he agreed with the move. MacDonald went six innings and gave up only one run — a good performance. Maybe a good omen.

"Phone call!" his sister shouted up the stairs.

"Who is it?" he hollered through the door.

"*I* don't know!" she said.

Downstairs, in the hallway, Gabriel picked up the extension. A voice said, "Ready for the tournament, big guy?"

"What tournament?"

"You think you're funny?" the voice said.

"Hey Andy," Gabriel said, surprising himself, "listen up, this is really weird. I gotta tell you something."

And then Andy, as if he knew what was coming, suddenly got quiet.

"It's about Pik."

Still nothing from Andy.

Gabriel waited. He didn't know how to say it, or even if he should say it.

"Andy, listen, I . . . Pik, uh . . . I saw him, in Recordland. This was a while ago. He didn't see me."

Silence.

Gabriel thought, he knows. "Andy, I don't know how to say this."

And then Andy said, "He was stealing records, right?"

"CDs," said Gabriel. And then he heard his voice crack, and he laughed nervously.

"I saw him take a CD. He slipped it inside his shirt."

"So Pik's a klepto?" Andy didn't sound upset. Just distant.

Gabriel shook his head. "I always knew he was spaced. Haven't I always told you that? Haven't I always told the Pikker that, to his face?"

"What're you gonna do?" Andy said.

"Look," Gabriel said. "It took me all this time just to tell *you*. I haven't done anything."

"You tell him you saw him?"

"No."

"Well," said Andy. And that was it.

Gabriel wasn't happy he'd brought it up at all. He didn't feel any better than when he was stewing about it, all by himself. Not any worse, but not any better.

By the time of the first tournament game, on

Saturday morning, it was as if Gabriel had never talked to Andy.

The first game was unexpectedly close, a rouser of a seesaw battle; the lead changed hands four or five times. Johnson went into the top of the ninth losing by two runs, and Gabriel's home run, with Andy on base, tied the score. Both teams played great defense for a couple of innings, and then Johnson scratched out a run in the top of the twelfth, Ray getting the RBI single. In the bottom of the inning, with a man on first, Pik dove to his left, snared a hard grounder and began a pretty double play that brought the parents in the bleachers to their feet. Then with two outs in the bottom of the twelfth, leading 7–6, a kid tripled. The next kid bunted, a perfect bunt. Gabriel couldn't believe it; he was sure he'd blown the lead. But Ronnie Duggan came out of his crouch faster than Gabriel thought possible and was up the third-base line, grabbing the ball bare-handed, tagging the runner out as he dove by.

Game over.

The team mobbed Duggan. Gabriel, Pik, and Andy joined in. They were going to the quarterfinals.

They ate lunch at Pik's. His dad grilled some hamburgers in their small backyard, spatula in one hand, can of beer in the other. Gabriel sat on the grass, spaced out and eating slowly, watching Pik's parents — The Zombies, Pik called them — dance around one another in the strange way they had; they were together, and yet somehow they weren't. "Ketchup?" Pik's dad would say to his mom, and she'd hand it to him. He'd take it, and during all of this, they'd never even look at each other. Andy nudged Gabriel at one point, and Gabriel looked up and saw them both standing beside the grill, plates in hand, eating — back-to-back; preferring, apparently, to stare into space rather than to talk to each other.

The afternoon was hot, and humid; the sun was a dull yellow disk in a hazy, washed-out sky. They barely made it to the second game on time, but at least Gabriel didn't have to take a long warm-up; he wasn't pitching. Mike MacDonald started; Gabriel played right field, Pik center: with MacDonald pitching, Coach Morris apparently expected all the action to be in the outfield.

The team from Trumbull was better than the team they'd played that morning, and right away they jumped all over Mike for three runs. Johnson then failed to score in their half of the first. The opposing pitcher was anything but overpowering, but he could get the ball over the plate, and Andy, Ray, Pik, and Gabriel were flat. Their legs were sore. Their arms felt like Play-Doh. Hamburgers sat heavy in their stomachs. They hit weak fly balls and grounders, and were out one, two, three.

For a few innings, the game continued in lack-luster fashion: mediocre pitching beating mediocre hitting. In the late innings, Johnson was still down 3–0.

Gabriel found himself sitting on the bench next to Duggan. At first he thought, if Duggan's not gonna talk, I'm not. Then he thought, wait a minute, I'm getting an attitude, too. Why not make an effort, talk to the guy? So Gabriel turned and looked at Duggan, who was sweating up a storm, and said, "That was a great play this morning."

Duggan shrugged.

"Saved *my* butt, I'll tell you that," Gabriel said.

Duggan nodded, still looking out at the field.

"You're about the only one who played great."

Duggan turned to him. His brown eyes looked straight at Gabriel. "You did," he said.

"Yeah, well . . ."

"Pik did. Andy, too."

"Well . . ." Gabriel was at a loss for words. "So?"

"So. You're wrong." Duggan turned his eyes back to the field.

Gabriel stared at him, noticing his hair hanging

over his ear, dark with perspiration, and the sweat-soaked collar of his uniform shirt. What could you say to a guy like that? Gabriel thought. When you tried to be friendly, he shoved it back in your face.

Again they hung on the verge of elimination. Trumbull, already ahead 3–0, threatened to widen the margin in the ninth: players on second and third, one out, their number-four hitter up. Coach Morris, in a surprisingly sensible frame of mind, and without his Walkman for once, trudged to the mound and waved Gabriel in from the outfield. He said to Mike, Andy, and Gabriel: "Guys, we lose this one, there's no tomorrow. No sense saving our ace in this spot, is there?"

Gabriel warmed up, got number four to pop-up, and struck out number five.

It turned the game around. Andy led off the bottom of the inning with a bunt single and stole second on the next pitch. Trumbull got nervous. They missed Gabriel's sharp grounder, and threw the ball away twice as Gabriel headed for second, then third. There was no throw home.

The rally continued and Trumbull fell apart as Ray doubled and Duggan drove him in, tying the score 3–3.

Now the five-through-nine hitters had two outs

to play with to get Duggan home. They didn't need them. Pik singled; Duggan rounded second without slowing down, and Coach Morris, left arm pinwheeling, right arm pointing, sent him home. The throw from short-right field was on-line, but it bounced just in front of the catcher, and as Duggan slid, the ball ricocheted off the kid's chest protector — and the game was over. They were still in it.

They ate dinner on the run, between games, standing around Pik's kitchen: three-bean salad and leftovers.

Pik's mother drove them to the next game in the rusty yellow Buick, which was miraculously running. Even more miraculously, she decided to stay and watch. Pik kept turning to stare in the direction where she was sitting, high up in the bleachers.

But Pik didn't have a chance to be distracted or to be a hero. The lights came on; the teams came out; and after a couple of innings, the outcome was clear: Johnson was going to score, the other team wasn't.

Still, Pik kept glancing over his shoulder, jiggling his foot. Gabriel was sitting on the bench next to Pik. It was early in the game. Robin Lenz was at bat; Andy was in the on-deck circle. Everybody on the Johnson side was loose, relaxed, enjoying themselves. There were a couple of guys on base.

"Dull," said Pik, turning around for about the hundredth time. "This game is *dull*."

"Parents never know the difference," offered Gabriel. Pik didn't answer.

"So why'd you do it?" Gabriel asked.

"Do what?"

"You know. The CDs, man."

"What CDs?"

"Why're you taking all those CDs?"

Cheers erupted from the bleachers, and Pik and Gabriel looked back out toward the diamond. Another run crossed the plate; there were high fives and laughter along the bench. It was 7–0. Andy walked out and settled himself in the batter's box.

"Why, Pik?" Gabriel persisted. "I saw you a while ago, out at Recordland. But I haven't told anybody. I just want to know."

"Juice one, Andy!" Pik hollered. Andy took strike one.

"Well," Gabriel said, "I guess you got your reasons."

"Oh really, you *guess* that?" Pik said. He looked sharply at Gabriel, startling him. "So go ahead, what are my reasons?"

"I don't know. You tell me."

Pik shook his head.

Andy lashed a line drive foul, past third. Coach did a little dance to keep from getting hit.

"I don't know why I do it," Pik said.

They watched Andy step out of the batter's box, pick up some dirt, and release it with little shakes of his hand.

"It's like, I keep thinking I'll get a CD player someday."

Gabriel worked the dirt with his spike. "You ask your folks for one?"

"Not yet. But I'll tell you this."

"What?"

"You're on deck, jerk." He elbowed Gabriel in the ribs.

Gabriel jumped to his feet just as Andy lined a pitch sharply between short and third.

Pik slapped his butt. "Crush it," he said.

The other team clearly had spent itself winning its first two games. Their pitcher was either exhausted or a bench warmer. He threw plenty of strikes, but most of them were right down the middle. In the third inning, Coach moved Gabriel to right field and brought in Tony Picarazzi to pitch; Johnson was up 9–0.

When it was finally over, everyone had played, and they had played well. They hadn't hot-dogged it; they'd played sound fundamental baseball with concentration and intensity. They were going to the finals.

But it wasn't clear yet who their opponent would be. On a nearby diamond, the other semifinal game was only in the fourth inning. Flood was down by two.

8.
Showdown

Flood won.

    Now it was Johnson and Flood.

The morning was perfect for baseball, blue sky and high cotton clouds, and a faint breeze with just enough coolness. But no one was basking in the perfect weather. No one was joking, no one was cutting up.

The Mantis was taking warm-up pitches. Flood was moving through its routine like a picture-perfect sports commercial; their uniforms were crisp, spotless, and matching; their motions precise. They didn't look like they'd been playing baseball nonstop for the last twenty-four hours. They didn't look like they'd ever even broken a sweat.

"I hate those guys," muttered Pik, lacing up his cleats — battered good-luck cleats — held together as much by the shoelaces wound twice around the insole, as anything else.

Andy said, unexpectedly, vehemently, "Me, too."

Pik bared his teeth, a Pik before-a-game grin. "That's the spirit, Android."

Gabriel grabbed his Louisville Slugger — and all the tar from the handle came off on his hands. He looked down at his gooey palms, stunned.

Laughter broke out from Andy's end of the dugout, spreading down the line through Ray, MacDonald, and Picarazzi.

"Hey!" said Gabriel. "What's this?"

"Marmite." Andy was practically rolling off the bench.

"What?"

"The English put it on toast," said Pik, in a really awful British accent.

"I'll put it on *your* toast." Gabriel headed for the dugout. But Andy was too quick, and Gabriel gave up. He started trying to wash the gook off in the water fountain.

"Lucky for you I'm saving myself for the game," he told Andy. "When we're finished with Flood, you die."

"See the fear in my eyes?" Andy said. "You missed a spot." He pointed.

"Okay team, listen up." Coach took both earphones out.

"Big game," muttered Pik, and twisted around a bit. Gabriel turned to follow Pik's gaze, then turned back and met Andy's eye and shrugged. Pik's mother was there again, alone at the top of the bleachers, staring out over the field.

"This is Flood. We've lost to them twice. Third time's the charm," Coach said. There was a long pause. Half the team turned to look at Pik, waiting for him to raise his hand. But Pik only bared his teeth again, and kept his hands down.

Flood batted first. Gabriel wound up, and put the first kid on his rear with a brushback pitch. Flood's coach was up and out of the dugout, but this umpire didn't even take his mask off. "Ball," he said in flat voice. "Play."

"Marmite meat," screamed Andy. Gabriel ignored him.

The kid overswung at the next pitch, and grounded out.

Okay, thought Gabriel.

The next kid was their starting pitcher from their first game. Gabriel called him the Dung Beetle. He got all of a wounded-duck curve and parked it over the fence in left.

Gabriel didn't even turn to watch him circle the bases. He stopped thinking altogether.

He struck out the number-three hitter with the fastball he should've thrown at Dung Beetle, and Duggan took out number four on a pop-up behind the plate.

It's a start, thought Gabriel as he watched Andy and Pik, walking in. But we have a long way to go.

They held Flood to that one run through the next three innings, and Flood held Johnson to zip. By the bottom of the fourth, everyone was frustrated.

"This is no way to win a ballgame," grumbled Pik, thumping his glove against Gabriel's butt as they walked off.

Duggan looked up. "Or lose one, either."

Gabriel returned Duggan's stare, coolly.

Andy caught that. He raised his head and watched Duggan walk into the dugout. But he didn't say anything.

Instead he led off with a hit to the deepest part of center field, barely giving Gabriel time to reach the on-deck circle. Gabriel toed in, watched one fat strike cross the plate, and then did the same as Andy, only farther. Home run. Three pitches, two runs.

The Flood coach went out to the mound to settle the Dung Beetle down. Whatever he said didn't work. Ray blasted a triple on the next pitch. Then Duggan singled Ray home, Pik singled, and that was all for the Dung Beetle.

The crowd gave him a hand as he left the mound with Flood's coach.

"What's the hand for?" Pik said from first base. "He faced five guys and they all got hits."

"Hey, Pik," Coach called from the dugout.

"Nice work," called Pik sarcastically. "What does that do to your ERA?"

"Lay off, Pik," Coach said.

"Yeah, I know," said Pik. "Summer league."

It wasn't the Mantis they sent in.

It was a mistake.

The new pitcher, somebody named MacManamy, threw five pitches to Mike MacDonald. Mike fouled off four and singled the fifth. Duggan scored.

Then Steve Wright singled into the gap, and Pik came home jumping on the plate like it was the seventh game of the World Series.

The score was 5–1.

Tony Picarazzi drove one all the way back to the warning track. It was caught, but the sacrifice moved everybody over. Robin Lenz popped up. Then Andy was up again. He hit a screamer, but the pitcher flagged it down from the mound.

"Self-defense," said Andy cheerfully as he trotted back for his glove.

Gabriel settled into a rhythm and struck out the side.

In the bottom of the fifth, Steve Wright singled again. But Tony Picarazzi wasn't able to move him over. Then Robin Lenz laid a soft bunt down first that stayed fair. He was gunned out, but Wright went to second.

"Take me out to the ballgame," sang Pik.

Gabriel shook his head. Pik was so wired today. Wired and weird.

Then the pitcher, who clearly wasn't in control, almost beaned Andy. Andy went down, got up. The umpire said in the same flat voice he'd used throughout the game, "Ball. Play ball." Andy lined the next one over the pitcher's head so close it probably brushed the top of the kid's hat.

Wright scored and Gabriel headed for the batter's box.

Looks like things are about to get out of hand, he thought happily.

But they didn't. Gabriel struck out, took the third strike with the bat on his shoulder.

"Nice play," grunted Duggan.

I could hit him with this bat, thought Gabriel. Naah. *Not yet.*

Behind Duggan, Andy said, "Score is 7–1. Let him live."

Gabriel took it out on Flood with exactly nine sizzling fast balls.

Duggan didn't say anything this time.

But Flood's coach sent the Mantis in at the bottom of the seventh.

"It's too late baby, baby, it's too late," sang Pik.

"Pik," said Coach.

"It's our secret weapon, coach," said Andy. "Pik sings, they'll do anything for him to stop."

"So will his own team," said Gabriel. "Andy, get out the marmite."

Pik stopped singing. Turned. Checked. Yeah, his mother was still there, sitting in the stands.

The Mantis answered Gabriel with nine strikes right back.

"Keep singing, Pik," muttered Gabriel, going out to the mound.

Flood got two runs off Johnson before their half of the inning was over. A couple of doubles and a bloop single.

Still, 7–3, bottom of the seventh, big deal.

But suddenly they were listless. Suddenly the sun felt too bright, the breeze a little cold. They were headed into error country, Gabriel could feel it.

He could feel it, but he couldn't do anything about it.

He watched as Ray singled to lead off, but then hesitated before trying to stretch it into a double and was thrown out. Ray? Hesitate? Then Duggan grounded out. Pik popped up.

And Flood came roaring back.

Gabriel wound up and threw, wound up and threw. When he'd finished, he'd thrown four balls and the number-nine batter was on first. He struck out their lead-off man, and then walked their number-two hitter. Then the Mantis came up, swung at junk, and singled into the right-field hole; the runner went home.

No one on Johnson said anything. No razzing, no chatter. It was like he was up there alone, just him and Flood.

Say something, Gabriel thought.

He walked the next guy.

Sing something, Gabriel thought.

Number five singled. And Gabriel walked number six.

The whole infield came to a conference on the mound.

Now they wanna talk, thought Gabriel disgustedly.

"What's going on?" Andy said, cuffing Gabriel on the cheek. Gabriel jerked his head away.

Duggan said, "Fixx, you blow this, I'll kill you myself."

Gabriel waited.

Everyone went back to their positions.

Thanks for the support, guys, Gabriel thought.

Coach still hadn't moved from the bench. He was watching them all with a sort of mild interest, almost as detached as Pik's mother.

Duggan called two straight curves, which Gabriel threw. The kid missed them both. Duggan called for a fastball, but Gabriel shook him off, and sent in another curve. The kid hit a line-drive foul.

Duggan stood up and stared at Gabriel for a minute.

All right, all right, thought Gabriel. When Duggan called for another fastball, Gabriel threw it and struck the kid out.

Now Coach stood up. He put one foot outside the dugout, and just stood there.

"Yea Coach," shouted Pik.

Duggan called for three straight curves and Gabriel bent the ball in beautifully, right to left, just at the kid's knees, each one a called strike.

Two outs now. Flood's coach waved the next batter back to the dugout. They were sending in a pinch hitter.

Ray, of all people, called time-out and jogged in to the mound from center field. Gabriel looked at him, letting his mouth drop open in exaggerated surprise.

Ray ignored it. "I know this kid," he said, as Duggan joined them, his mask on his head. "His name is Chandler. Don't throw him a curve, under any circumstances. Curves are his meat. He hasn't met one yet, he didn't turn around."

"He hasn't met mine," said Gabriel.

"*Don't* do it," Ray said, and left.

"Do what?" asked Coach, getting there too late.

"Lose the game," said Duggan, giving Gabriel a hard look. He snapped his mask down and went back to the plate.

"Good luck, son," said Coach.

Thanks a lot, thought Gabriel.

Fastball, signalled Duggan.

Steamed, Gabriel threw it faster. Two outs, bases loaded, strike one.

Fastball.

Gabriel aimed, but he wasted it outside — 1 and 1.

Fastball. The kid tipped it — 1 and 2.

Fastball.

Gabriel shook him off. Duggan shook Gabriel off, and called time-out, again.

"Move it," said the ump.

Duggan hustled out, stopped. "Don't do this, Fixx."

"Do what?" said Gabriel. "Throw a strike?"

"Don't do it," repeated Duggan. He went back, crouched down, signalled for a fastball.

Gabriel threw a curve. The kid barely fouled it off.

The guy can hit any curve, huh, DeVellis? He gave Duggan a big smile.

Duggan signalled for a fastball. Gabriel shook him off. Duggan called for a fastball again, but Gabriel was already in his windup. He let it go, knowing it was a wicked breaking ball, knowing it was a strikeout.

Chandler took it squarely in his wheelhouse, and gave it a ride into blue infinity.

Flood, 8–7.

This, thought Gabriel, is the worst moment of my life.

Coach mimed a question from the dugout. Gabriel waved it off with a numb arm.

I could die, thought Gabriel.

He worked the next batter for a while, finally got him out. He took a deep breath, stepped off the mound, and walked toward the dugout.

"You mucus," said Duggan. "Snot. Toe cheese."

"Yo," said Pik. "Coach says we gotta act like a team, Duggan. Get it?"

Duggan glared at Pik, then shrugged. "It'd help to play like a team."

Ray didn't say anything, didn't even look Gabriel's way. But Andy and Pik sat down on either side of him.

"Kim, Fixx, DeVellis," said Pik. "That's the lineup. What more can we ask for?"

Andy picked up his bat, headed out for the plate. "Marmite it!" said Pik.

"Good, Pik," said Coach. "Let's have some chatter, let's have some talk. C'mon Andy. Home run now!"

Pik rolled his eyes.

The Mantis threw a curve; Andy swung and missed. Then he fouled two more off. Finally, he dribbled one toward the shortstop, flew down the line, and was safe by a step.

Gabriel, taking a practice swing, heard Duggan's voice.

"Hit it and live," Duggan shouted.

The Mantis took a breath. He took off his cap, discolored around the visor with sweat, and put it on again, continuing to stare at Gabriel.

The Mantis pitched. Gabriel swung. And missed.

"Strike one," said the ump, sounding bored.

"Wait for your pitch, jerk," Pik called helpfully.

Gabriel watched the next ball cross the plate.

"Ster-rike two," said the ump.

The Mantis stepped in. He threw. Gabriel lifted the bat, wavered. Yes . . . No . . . No.

"Ball one."

The Mantis waited, and then cut loose with another curve. Gabriel stepped into it, swung, and connected. Solid; not home run wood, but enough. Two men on, first and second, no outs.

"C'mon Ray," whispered Gabriel, ignoring the first baseman, ignoring the crescendo of sound from the bleachers.

Ball one. Ball two. And then a wicked curve that Ray belted. Andy took off. Gabriel took off.

And then, out of nowhere, the center fielder was under it. He caught it, and threw it before Andy could even begin to turn.

Gabriel dove for first as the second baseman

made the put-out on Andy, history repeating itself.

Ray stood there. Then he dropped the bat and walked away. Two outs.

Duggan was up. He didn't even looked bothered. He stood there, cocking the bat.

The Mantis burned one in close to Duggan's ear. Duggan turned his head like it was a fly; annoying, but no big deal.

"Ball one," called the umpire.

I hate this game, thought Gabriel, leaning off the base.

The next pitch was perfect, an apple, ready for shining. Duggan watched it, and as the ump called, "Strike one," he stepped out of the box and tapped his cleats with the bat.

He stepped back to the plate and dug in again.

The Mantis pulled back and fired. Duggan smiled. And Gabriel took off.

The crack of the bat was the best sound he ever heard. He put his head down and ran. He slammed a foot on each base he rounded and tried not to touch the ground in between. Head down, he felt, rather than saw, the Coach's wildly windmilling arms; he felt, rather than heard, the wave of sound breaking over the field. He didn't stop running until he hit the backstop fence with his shoulder, turning, trying to see if Duggan had done it — if Duggan was the hero.

It was in the park. It had gone off the fence, taking a wild hop coming back; the center fielder was relaying it in as Duggan was rounding third.

"Faster, faster," Pik was screaming.

"Go, go, go," Coach was shouting.

"C,monnnn," panted Gabriel. "C'mmon. . . ."

The shortstop threw. The Mantis ducked, and the ball streaked toward the catcher's glove.

Duggan began to slide.

It was the longest slide in the history of the universe.

Gabriel stopped breathing. The catcher strained forward, caught the ball, and swung around. One-tenth of a second too late.

In dirt, in dust, and in glory, Ronnie Duggan slid home.

The final score was Flood 8, Johnson 9.

They poured out of the dugout and mobbed each other. Pik lifted Lenz in the air, sidearmed MacDonald, and pounded on anyone he could reach. Andy and Ray got locked in a weird bunny hop across the infield, crashing into the mob. Even Coach got into the act, raising his arms, spraying a can of Coke he'd gotten from somewhere all over everyone.

Gabriel moved away from the backstop as the Mantis finished his long walk off the field. The guy looked exhausted. His cap was soaked. His hair was dripping. Gabriel stuck his hand out. "Good game."

"It was," the Mantis answered, but he didn't put his hand out. He smiled. "We'll see you guys again," he said. And he left.

Pik was dancing with his arms up, facing the bleachers. Gabriel looked up and saw Pik's mother actually standing up, applauding.

Pushing through the melee, Gabriel made his way to Duggan.

"Hey," he said. Duggan turned, more expression on his face than Gabriel had ever seen. "Nice hit."

Gabriel didn't offer to shake hands this time, and neither did Duggan. But he nodded. "Good game," he said.

"Yeah," replied Gabriel. "Good game."

Andy was coming toward him as he turned, grinning. Gabriel felt his own grin spreading. He loved it, he loved this game. This is why I play, he thought, *this* is why. He slung an arm around Pik, and high-fived Ray; and it was only after he'd brought his hand down that he remembered. He saw Andy cracking up, and felt Pik shaking with laughter. He remembered one crucial thing: All over his hand. Sticky. The marmite.

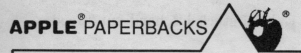